Copyright © 1997 by Nord-Süd Verlag AG, Gossau Zürich, Switzerland
First published in Switzerland under the title *Hase Hannes der Postbote*
English translation copyright © 1997 by North-South Books Inc.
All rights reserved. No part of this book may be reproduced or utilized
in any form or by any means, electronic or mechanical, including
photocopying, recording, or any information storage and retrieval
system, without permission in writing from the publisher.
First published in the United States, Great Britain, Canada,
Australia, and New Zealand in 1997 by North-South Books,
an imprint of Nord-Süd Verlag AG, Gossau Zürich, Switzerland.
Distributed in the United States by North-South Books Inc., New York.
Library of Congress Cataloging-in-Publication Data is available.
A CIP catalogue record for this book is available from The British Library.
ISBN 1-55858-687-3 (trade binding) 10 9 8 7 6 5 4 3 2 1
ISBN 1-55858-688-1 (library binding) 10 9 8 7 6 5 4 3 2 1
Printed in Belgium
For more information about our books, and the authors and artists
who create them, visit our web site: http://www.northsouth.com

Harvey Hare
Postman Extraordinaire

By Bernadette Watts

North-South Books
New York · London

Harvey Hare was a postman. Day after day, all year long, he carried the heavy mail bag far and wide, across the fields, up the hill and down the other side, delivering the mail to all the animals.

Harvey carried all sorts of mail—letters and parcels, birthday cards and invitations. One day he even delivered little bundles of twigs that had been sent to all the sparrows.

No matter what the season, no matter what the weather, Harvey made sure the mail was delivered.

When summer came and the hot sun beat down, Harvey walked more slowly across the fields—and even more slowly up the hill. He stopped in the shade of a cornfield to wipe his brow. Then he gave the field mouse a letter from the town mouse.

By the time Harvey delivered Hedgehog's mail it was high noon, the hottest time of the day! He was sweating, but there was still more mail to be delivered, so Harvey trudged on.

In autumn, the wind blew the leaves all around. It blew in Harvey's ears, and sometimes it even blew the letters out of his bag so Harvey had to chase after them. But Harvey made sure that the package for Mole didn't blow away, for Mole had sent for some spectacles to help improve her poor vision.

In late autumn came the storms. Heavy rain poured down on Harvey, soaking him to the skin. At night, when he returned home to his family sitting cozily in their hollow, Harvey was so wet it took him a whole hour to get dry!

When winter came, so did the snow. But that didn't stop Harvey. With snowflakes tickling his ears and nose, he hopped through the drifts, delivering letters and packages—and even a bag of nuts for Squirrel.

Badger's house was the last stop on Harvey's route. He staggered up the hill through the blinding snow to deliver his last letter. Badger invited him in for a cup of hot tea, which made Harvey feel better. Finally, with thanks to the kindly badger, Harvey headed home. He shook the snow from his fur, snuggled down in his hollow, and dreamed of spring.

One winter night, when the moon was full, Badger called
a meeting of the animals.

"Harvey Hare brings our mail through rain, and wind and
sun. We should give him a present to thank him," Badger said.

The other animals agreed. Squirrel had a great idea for the perfect gift. "But we'll have to wait until spring to find all the things we'll need to make it," Squirrel said.

Finally it was spring. Meadows and trees grew green. Flowers bloomed. The animals collected leaves and twigs, flowers and grasses to make the thank-you present for Harvey Hare. They all worked hard and soon it was finished.

"Surprise! Surprise!" the animals called. "Hooray for Harvey Hare, postman extraordinaire!"

Harvey was indeed surprised—and absolutely delighted with his present. "Thank you all," said Harvey. "This umbrella is just what I need!"

From then on Harvey took his umbrella
with him whenever he delivered the mail.
It protected him from the autumn winds, the
winter snow, the springtime showers, and the
hot summer sun. And when he had finished
making his deliveries, he would stretch out
in the shade of his beautiful umbrella and
enjoy a well-earned rest.